In loving memory of
Charles A. Tennant, Jr.
(1916-2010)

Blueberry Man

Story © Christina E. Petrides
Illustrations and design © Nika Tchaikovskaya

Publisher: Tchaikovsky·Family·Books
Republic of Korea, Jeju Island, Gujwa Eup, Deokcheondong-gil, 79
e-mail: tyfamilybooks@gmail.com
www.tyfamilybooks.myportfolio.com
instagram: @jeju_draw

ISBN 979-11-966402-2-4
First Edition, 2020
Set in Alphabetized Cassette Tapes Regular - a typeface licensed for this print edition from Brittney Murphey Design
Printed in South Korea by Sinsago Hi-tech.Co., Ltd

Christina E. Petrides

BLUEBERRY MAN

illustrated by Nika Tchaikovskaya

My Granddaddy was the Blueberry Man.

He had short white hair
   that stuck straight up
and twinkling blue eyes
   with crinkles at the corners.

He drove a big old sky-blue truck with rounded fenders.

He had a farm

with no cows,

no pigs,

and no chickens,

but several rows of corn,

some peas,

some cantaloupes...

and lots

and LOTS

of blueberry bushes.

Many years ago, he carefully planted
more than one hundred tiny blueberry bushes,

and he watered each

under the hot Georgia sun.

Over time,
the small bushes grew and grew,
leafy and healthy,
until each was taller than Granddaddy,
and almost as wide as his truck.

And every June and July,
there were thousands
and thousands of berries on them.

The ripe blueberries
were fat and round as marbles,

the color of the uniform
Granddaddy had worn in the Navy
when he was a young man.

He still had the uniform.

When his ship was hit by a torpedo
in the warm South Pacific,
he had waded through chest-deep water
to get it from his locker.

It had also traveled with him
to the icy North Atlantic,
where he had made

emergency repairs

to his ship

while it was hunted
by enemy submarines.

Once every year,
he would slip on the uniform coat,
which still fit,
and remember his shipmates
who hadn't come back from the war.

He told us grandchildren many stories about the faraway places he had visited and the interesting people he had met while he was in the Navy.

We picked bucketfuls of blueberries.

We also ate handfuls of blueberries
until our tongues and lips and fingers
were stained purple.

But that was OK. "Blueberries are good for you!"
Granddaddy said. "You can never have too many."

Grandmommy baked fresh blueberry muffins for breakfast.

She made blueberry pie and blueberry cobbler for dessert.

She packed neat bags
of blueberries
into the freezer
on the back porch.

She made blueberry jelly and blueberry jam
and put it in glass jars in the pantry.

Granddaddy
never sold his blueberries.

He always said,
"These blueberries are ONLY for family!"

But, in fact...

he gave them away to anyone he liked.

So, his blueberry family
included many, many people
we didn't really know.

They all called him the

Today, my aunt and uncle live on the farm.

They carefully water the blueberry bushes
while their own grandchildren play
where the corn and peas and cantaloupes once grew.

Every summer,
my aunt and uncle
invite our whole family
and all their friends
and all our friends
to come pick
blueberries.

And as we enjoy those thousands
and thousands and thousands of blueberries,
we remember my Granddaddy,

the Blueberry Man.

Christina E. Petrides is an American writer, poet, longtime blogger, and English teacher.
She earned a BA in Russian Studies from Washington and Lee University, an MA in International Studies
from the University of South Carolina (Columbia), and an MA in Russian History from Georgetown University.
From Columbia County, Georgia, she moved to Jeju Island, South Korea, in 2017.
Blueberry Man is her first children's book.

Nika Tchaikovskaya is a Russian illustrator, watercolor artist, and author.
She graduated from St. Petersburg Academy of Fine Arts and has worked as an illustrator
of educational and children's publications for over 20 years. She has been living on Jeju Island since 2013
and is the author and illustrator of the 해녀리나 picturebook series dedicated to Jeju women divers.

Printed with Saphira Eco : Non IPA
HEIDELBERG

PRINTED WITH
SOY INK

With people and the environment in mind, this book was printed using alcohol-free, plant-based ink.